2/15/24

Translated from the original:
ONE-INCH PUNCH FICTION

"The stories in *Translated from the Original: One-inch Punch Fiction* give us glimpses of what is overlooked, those things that are in front of us that illuminate the brightest of lights if we'd only look. These stories give us the unexpected, landing in places they are meant to — heart, spirit, mind. As the old boxing adage says, it's the punch you don't see that knocks you out. These stories are punches that come from unexpected angles that do not knock us out but knock us into life with new clarity among its complexities and contradictions."

Tony Robles
author of *Cool Don't Live Here No More—*
A Letter To San Francisco

"As the title implies, these little stories pack a wallop. Guy Biederman sheds a soft golden light on scenes of everyday life, illuminating their sublime and often surreal aspects. He's a writer of gentle revolutions, launching quietly thoughtful grenades into our psyche, verbal pyrotechnics that bloom like calming fractals. The Bard of Sausalito's quill is dipped in liquid hope. His tales are written in the script of kindness, alternating between spirits of stoic peace and experimental playfulness. *Translated From the Original: One-inch Punch Fiction* constructs a literary landscape wherein autobiographical fact mirrors dreamlike fiction, opening windows into brief moments of existence that unravel infinitely. This collection is American Zen, offering serenity, empathy, and dare I say it in these callous times—*love!*—a contemplative respite from the world's chaos."

J. Martin Strangeweather
author of *Poems from the Future Artopia*,
Chief Executive Prognosticator and Director of Thaumaturgic Research for the Santa Ana Literary Association

"In Guy Biederman's *Translated From the Original: One-inch Punch Fiction*, each story feels like a small stone dropped into the mind where the human ripples spread. Encompassing themes such as love and loss, forgiveness and redemption, often punctuated by cats and coffee, these wonderful pieces are worth many readings. What mostly draws me to this author's flash fiction is the effortless way he achieves his art. I admire the powerful way he reaches a reader on many levels and how the stories stand for more than themselves."

Meg Pokrass
Founding Editor of *Best Microfiction*,
and author of *Spinning to Mars*

"In these compact fictions a cast of memorable characters grapple with the questions that besiege us all as we crest the mountain of midlife and begin making our way down the other side. Who were we once and—perhaps more importantly—who and what are we capable of being now? The primacy of human connection, the power that language holds over our lives, the aftermath of trauma. Biederman deftly tempers these heady themes with moments of beauty and humor, with speculative elements, and even with the simple grace of a purring cat, an ocean breeze, or jazz pouring through the speakers. What a pleasure to be invited into a world where characters strive to shape their desired existence and where readers, by extension, are invited to do the same."

Veronica Montes
author of *The Conquered Sits at the Bust Stop, Waiting*
and *Benedicta Takes Wing & Other Stories*

"When one begins reading this collection, it is easy to slip into the settings, scenes, and assume the world being presented through a flow of image, sound, motion, and meaning. Guy tells stories, with stories between the lines, and even words, sometimes. His style is wonderfully complex; I'd say it has a cinemascopic perspective, which carefully directs the mind's eye, your insights, and the heart's trace, bringing to life a raft of your own memories or considerations upon which the imagination travels. Enjoy this beautifully created series of portraits, landscapes, histories, life humor, and well crafted words of a fine poet."

Dan Brady
longtime San Francisco poet
and curator of Sacred Grounds Open mic

"Biederman's wry pieces are at once absurd and charming, and that gives him an opening for truly moving insights about the human condition. It's a cliché to say 'you'll laugh, you'll cry,' but in so many of these gems you'll be doing both...at the same time."

Kevin Brennan
author of *Parts Unknown* and *The Prospect*,
editor of The Disappointed Housewife

"Biederman's book is a treasure of intimate, quotidian moments written as though we were the subject of his stories. Who cannot identify with having a cat on one's lap, eating cheesecake, and listening to jazz? Forget your definition of 'fiction.' All of these stories are true to the heart of who we are as members of the human race."

Jim Woessner
short story writer

"In impressionistic, surrealistic, lyrical prose, and plain language, Guy Biederman brilliantly exposes everything in this collection. The truths, lies, complications, and absurdities we all experience as we stumble through life, always thinking our secrets are unique and hidden. How delightful to find ourselves and how un-alone we are."

Joyce Bailey
Director of the Black Women's
Writer's Institute

"I knew better. I should have taken the stories in this collection slow, like a box of chocolates, savoring each tasty morsel, basking in the afterglow. But instead, I went all fangirl glutton and gobbled through like a fiend. Good thing it's Low Fat. Because now I'm going back and thoughtfully sampling one story at a time—the transitioning loves, the smug cats, the clueless dogs, the humorous and sometimes painful self-discoveries—delicious and flavorful alternative fictions that melt in your mind like truth."

Linda Saldaña
Writer at Large

"Biederman's love for writing, his unabashed belief in its ordinary magnificence, infects, while his stories punch with equanimity, humor, and devastation. Biederman is a master but one you'll want to hang out with, hurt with, and bump down the river with, just as his sentences seem to, only when you arrive at their destination you know you arrived via a deeply intelligent and compassionate guide. Biederman is heart, play, America, and nothing but the real-deal—an original in any language."

Kara Vernor
author of *Because I Wanted to Write*
You a Pop Song

"In Guy Biederman's *Translated From the Original: One-inch Punch Fiction*, form follows function around the house like a cat seeking the sunbaked corner. It settles there, then stretches and moves on to the next paragraph. Or story Biederman is a writer's writer. You can feel him paying attention. Metaphor is the light and the one-inch punch that illuminates everything and wakes us up, knocks us out. He is crafty, as he translates concrete everyday narrative—the original?—abruptly, into word-art. Nostalgia and harsher memory might be the portals for this magic.

Writing is clearly Biederman's religion, alongside Judeo-Christian punishment and a sometimes ironic striving after Buddhist reconciliation. His themes reach toward light and dark; memory and loss (of memory); detachment/engagement; discovery/more loss/recovery; violence and peace. He leaves his .22 near the meditation bench, because carrying it around 'could be awkward.' These pieces are full of a carefully balanced grace. Enjoy. Reflect. Come back for another round."

Norma Smith
author of *Home Remedy*

NOMADIC PRESS

OAKLAND

PHILADELPHIA

XALAPA

WWW.NOMADICPRESS.ORG

MASTHEAD

FOUNDING PUBLISHER
J. K. Fowler

ASSOCIATE EDITOR
Michaela Mullin

LEAD EDITOR
Nina Sacco

DESIGN
Jevohn Tyler Newsome

MISSON STATEMENT Through publications, events, and active community participation, Nomadic Press collectively weaves together platforms for intentionally marginalized voices to take their rightful place within the world of the written and spoken word. Through our limited means, we are simply attempting to help right the centuries' old violence and silencing that should never have occurred in the first place and build alliances and community partnerships with others who share a collective vision for a future far better than today.

INVITATIONS Nomadic Press wholeheartedly accepts invitations to read your work during our open reading period every year. To learn more or to extend an invitation, please visit: www.nomadicpress.org/invitations

DISTRIBUTION
Orders by teachers, libraries, trade bookstores, or wholesalers:

Nomadic Press Distribution
orders@nomadicpress.org
(510) 500-5162

Small Press Distribution
spd@spdbooks.org
(510) 524-1668 / (800) 869-7553

This book was made possible by a loving community of chosen family and friends, old and new. For author questions or to book a reading at your bookstore, university/school, or alternative establishment, please send an email to info@nomadicpress.org.

Cover art: "untitled map no. 13-11" by Thérèse Murdza

Author portrait by Arthur Johnstone

Published by Nomadic Press, 1941 Jackson Street, Suite 20, Oakland, CA 94612

First printing, 2022

Library of Congress Cataloging-in-Publication Data

Title: ***Translated From The Original: One-inch Punch Fiction***
p. cm.
Summary: Influenced by Sonny Rollins and Thelonius Monk, powered by chi, inspired by Bruce Lee, *Translated From The Original: One-inch Punch Fiction* weaves through lines of love, loss, pain, discovery, and redemption, with dollops of whimsy and notes of wonder. Biederman's genre-bending collection of flash and micro fiction is a book you'll want to share with friends, but may hesitate to lend. Better get two.

[1. FICTION / Micro. 2. FICTION / Nature & the Environment. 3. FICTION / Short Stories (single author). 4. FICTION / General.]

LIBRARY OF CONGRESS CONTROL NUMBER: 2022944579

ISBN:978-1-955239-34-9

Translated from the original:

ONE-INCH
PUNCH
FICTION

Translated from the original:

ONE-INCH
PUNCH
FICTION

GUY BIEDERMAN

**NOMADIC
PRESS**

Oakland · Philadelphia · Xalapa

"I realized by using the high notes of the chords as a melodic line,
and by the right harmonic progression, I could play what I heard inside me.
That's when I was born."

CHARLIE PARKER

For Phyllis

and

*in memory
of Will*

CONTENTS

I.

II.

III.

NOTES
READING GUIDE

FOREWORD

When Guy asked me to write the foreword for *Translated From The Original: One-inch Punch Fiction*, I instinctively responded with an enthusiastic "Yes, absolutely!"

After all, I'm a writer who loves to write, and another writer had just asked me to write something—woo-hoo! There's also the added pleasure of having known Guy and, more to the point, having been familiar with his writing for more than twenty-five years.

I suppose, with that pleasure, there might've been pressure, too, since Guy and I are friends. But if such pressure existed, I can honestly say I never felt it. Guy is an expert craftsman and I'm an unabashed admirer—that's the plain straightforward unvarnished honest truth, and I'm sticking with all those adjectives because that's my style, the rhythm with which I prefer to effect literary self-expression. It's not Guy's. We write about different things in different ways, and that's ok. Guy makes every word count and, in my reading of his stories, his fine-tuned word choices usually count for more than one emotion, or more than one experience; or, coincidentally, more than one inter-pretation—or translation, as the case may be. Several of Guy's stories transcend the realm of the superbly crafted and reach the high altitude of art, this collection's eponymous story being one example, and "Lovers of a Bygone Era" being another, to name just two.

The art of flash fiction, or micro fiction, or whatever label you choose to stick on this collection is, of course, a reader's joy to behold.

Guy, like me, resists getting caught up in that sort of semantic debate. But the craft in every story—so consistent, so perfectly polished, so masterfully accomplished—that's where my deepest appreciation abides.

But I will say this: Don't play poker with Guy Biederman.

Why?

Because if Guy plays poker the way he writes what one publisher calls his "lyrical micro-prose," you're going to get taken, time and time again.

But in a good way.

A very good way.

While you're reading any of Guy's stories in this marvelously entertaining collection, at first you're likely to think, oh, this is a gently whimsical story about, say, a car-crowded distinctly un-Kerouac road trip or the creation of the universe or how dodgy a dog park can be or a hitchhiking seabird or playing pickup basketball or a cat with editing skills or protecting koi from "juvenile delinquents with claws" or shop-lifting in a bookstore or the high holy delight of smelling freshly baked cookies. Or any brief meditation on the seemingly quotidian.

But then, upon finishing each story, you're going to think, whoa, that was intense and insightful, or that was thought-provoking, or that was about self-esteem or humility or pride or friendship or making a bad decision or making a personal declaration of independence or discovering disturbing truths about oneself.

What Guy does, and does so smartly, is set a trap for the reader, not unlike the narrator in the nonpareil "The Trap," setting one for a raccoon, except Guy's traps aren't fatal; in fact they're inner-life enriching.

But the reader doesn't realize it, not right away, often not until the last sentence, occasionally not until the final phrase.

That's when the reader understands what great good fortune it is to be so trapped, ever so briefly, in Guy's imagination.

And what a rich, multilayered, and particularly big-hearted imagination it is.

Robert Eugene Rubino
author of *Aficionado: Poetry and Prose
Influenced By Cinema, Sports and Jazz*

INTRODUCTION

T*ranslated From The Original: One-inch Punch Fiction* explores how things transform, how they evolve from where they were to perhaps where they are now. It champions the big power of small things, the enormous impact of a tiny action or thought or idea or gesture or story.

I went under the hood for this new work all day and into the 2:00 am night, blending the rhythms of jazz and the chi of kung fu, specifically Thelonious Monk, Johnny Hodges, Sonny Rollins, and Roland Kirk, with Bruce Lee's Jeet Kune Do, 'style of no style', and the surge and burst of his one-inch punch. The parallels of structure and tone between jazz and these micro-grooves intrigue me, as well as the astonishing power generated by a one-inch punch, and by a one- or two- or three-page story.

Some of these micros were translated from their original forms as poems. Genre, like gender, can be fluid, can itself evolve. For many years I practiced a craft called low-fat fiction, a form that draws its power from what is left out. Working as a gardener, I saw the connections between bonsai and what I was trying to do on the page – the space between the branches, the space between the lines, defining the structure that remained. And something else. The short form allows for what I call The Reader's Art, leaving space for the reader to bring their imagination to the encounter, to participate in the exchange, and make the shared experience their own as well. This is one way to make a small story larger without more words, one way to extend the painting beyond the frame.

My hope is that you are moved by my work, that these micros and flash invite you in and inspire you to relish your own craft as a reader in a shared sphere of imagination, and perhaps discover connections to other crafts you practice as well, whatever those grooves they may be.

It's all true, especially the fiction.

Guy Biederman

THE WRITING LAID DOWN LIKE STEPS OF STONE

Mirabel's mom was not a writer. But in the days weeks months before she died, she couldn't stop writing. She wrote in the margins of the phone book, in the gutter of the daily news, on the covers of first editions in tiny nonsensical cursive, all the words connected. Curious fever. Channel of enlightenment. Flame reaching beyond fever and fury, and well-meaning fact that always fell short, or perhaps beyond our understanding.

This is what we know of Mirabel's mom, whom we never met, but remember from stories 10 years back. Mirabel making trips to Ohio to check-in, visit as her mother diminished, contracted, and expanded. This is what we know of Mirabel's mom, who died alone, as we work backward. A puzzle. A person. A life threaded by words. The writing laid down like steps of stone on a path all her own, the path Mirabel's mom, not a writer, followed until her last word. That is to say, her last step, a long and final breath being her only punctuation.

TURN ON THE A/C

Traveling cross country, we were four kids plus a friend, a mom, a dad, a grandma, and a dog in the family Falcon wagon, with our luggage strapped on top and a canvas bag of water stretched across the grill. Dad sat behind the wheel with his twitches and tics and Maalox, dreaming of a Galaxy with four on the floor and a beehive blonde named Nadine in a bucket seat beside him, his life a country-western song—*Devil Woman* specifically.

Somewhere near Odessa on the way to Huntsville, someone realized they'd left me back at the Stuckey's, where we'd stopped for gas and date shakes. They had to turn around. I imagined some debate arose from whoever had taken my seat in the way back; Mom scolding Dad, Susie the old collie looking worried, and Grandma stoic, her mind 60 years back, jumping off the train in the middle of the night, middle of nowhere, to get away from the old German.

I watched them load up and leave without me as I ducked behind the Frito stand. I hated dates. I ordered my own chocolate shake, feeling rich with the fiver I'd saved from collecting bottles, and looking back towards California, where I figured my thumb could take me, as I waited by the Interstate for a Camaro or maybe a Nova, with A/C and more legroom going my way.

HOW MONDAY
WAS MADE

It's been a rough day. Ice Age in the morning, Vesuvius after lunch, and the loss of God's favorite trattoria in Pompeii . . .

God rolls a joint, invents the match, and fires up around 5:00, though a fanatical cadre of historians would later insist it was 4:20 and took place in San Rafael, California, and not Eden, Garden of. Whatever, it's hard to leave work at the office. Obsessing about that pill, Ghengis Khan, and what went wrong, God creates the Cosmo and the cocktail glass for good measure.

After the second drink, God sees that it's all good. Very good. Very all good.

The world's a beautiful place. Even the cocktail glass is awesome. God's an overachiever, picked by no one to go this far until others were created, jumped on the bandwagon, and started singing his praises. Figures.

God gets the munchies. Invents M&M's, Newman's popcorn, and Ben & Jerry's Cherry Garcia. Having missed out on The Dead due to distractions like Bangladesh, the Beatles, and Marlin Perkins on Mutual of Omaha's Wild Kingdom, God re-discovers Jerry Garcia. Becomes a deadhead for a day. Supposedly stays away from the Owsley acid, though skeptics in Quebec point to the '89 solar storm that sent compasses spinning as evidence God may have dropped a tab or two at the Montreal show.

The yellow moon rises in the purple sky, and God, longing for a best friend, creates the basset whose goofy looks bring on a grin.

"I'll call you Absurd," says God.

"I'll call you a turd," replies the basset.

They laugh and discover they are the mirror image of one another. God is dog spelled backward, and dog is god. And God is good when you add an o. "Oh," says Absurd. " Good God, we're good . . . dog."

God dozes in the Adirondack. His snores flow into thunder. A screeching owl sails low in the velvety sky, and the Bassett knows his new best friend is dreaming. Lifting his mighty snout, the hound cuts loose a mournful howl that echoes off canyon walls and returns as a breeze —a wind—a tropical storm.

God awakes grumpy, rarely a good thing. And just like that, Monday is made.

SONNY ROLLINS AND SCRAMBLED EGGS

Listening to Sonny Rollins and eating scrambled duck eggs for lunch, I witness a lipstick collision on the corner of Gate 5 Road and Bridge. Clearing my plate, I locate an errant slice of cheesecake in the fridge and do the honors. Damn, it's good with cold milk. Out the houseboat window, that collision's been cleared. It was nobody's fault; no numbers exchanged, no witnesses except for one old dude eating cake and listening to jazz on the other side of streaked glass. And he didn't see a thing. Apparently.

I rinse my cup and say, Alexa off, but she's diggin' the tenor sax, so I say, Fuck it, and she says, Affirmative. I roll on down to the Church of Lift, do some curls, some bench, some ab work but on the 23rd situp, I realize the cheesecake was a very bad idea, in no uncertain terms. I call it a day, head back to the boat feeling scrambled myself.

Three ducks float by the pier. Maybe it was the eggs. I open the portal, and Alexa's moved on to Bach. I say, Alexa, play Thelonious Monk. She says she doesn't know the Loneliest Monk, and I say, What the fuck, over, and she says, Roger that, out.

Through the window, I witness runaway mascara streaking down Gate 5 toward Bridge. That's one happening intersection. I find my chair, and the cat finds me. So does Monk, as Alexa cues *Straight No Chaser*. As usual, it's just what the doctor ordered.

REFOLDING THE MAP

Teresa pops open the glove box of her father's Ford Fiesta with a soft punch and sifts through the jumble inside: pocketknife, stick of Dentyne, dead flashlight, registration, California map. Hairbrush. She grins. He was bald. She ponders the puffs of dark hair between the tines.

Her father's marbled hands with their tattoo of veins and contour of broken knuckles had once touched these objects, had once placed each item here. The old map is soft and worn. She spreads it open on the hood, warm to the touch from the Tucson sun.

A thick pink line runs from Ventura up the coast to the Redwoods. She pictures the travel clerk at AAA highlighting the route for her dad. That trip, so far away, so long ago. Driving through the Giant Redwood that bridged the road. Testing balance at Gravity Hill. Eating hot dogs on the Lost Coast. Lost, almost.

She once read how cartographers create fictional roads on their maps to protect against infringement. She wonders what might happen were travelers to stumble upon such a fictional route. Would they sojourn for a spell in the same shared sphere of imagination?

She gazes across the desert. Smells salt air. Sees her father's blue-grey eyes in the color of distant sage. Smiles at the tumbleweed hair of his highway youth. Teresa refolds her father's map, easily following its deeply creviced folds. She returns his map to the glove box and feels the door close with a gentle click.

G

You found the letter G in your shirt pocket. 12 point. Times New Roman. Didn't think much of it until you tried to hit the __round runnin__.

Decided to stay home and fix coffee instead.

"Hey," said a nei__hbor pounding on the wall. "Did you hear? A letter's missin__."

Others in the complex started whinin__, too. Like a blackout or somethin__.

"Hey," said your wife __ina. "Look what happened to my name!"

You fin__ered the letter in your pocket, pretended to sympathize. After all, you'd lost a first letter, too.

Your __ay brother called, said he was adding an e and becoming a pirate.

"Aye, aye?" You asked.

"Ar__h!" he answered.

Your mutt __uido took to the name chan__e, too. Started putting on forei__n airs. __uido?? Sounded Bushido or somethin__

. . .

__ina moped a bit and watched __eraldo on TV. But he didn't

care, his __ was silent anyway. Your name, on the other hand, had become unpronounceable: __uy.

Ima__ine havin__ a name that even you can't say. Talk about feelin__ invisible.

People adapt to loss, or so you've been told.

The sun rose.

You tried to eschew words that used the 7th letter, but when you __limpsed the fiery sky, it slipped out. "How __lorius."

__ina, not a church __oer, murmured, " __lory be to __od."

Odd? It hit you. You weren't the only one with name issues. And if the Bi __ __uy wanted his old name back, he knew where to look.

Nonchalantly, you stuffed your shirt in a ba__ and headed off to __ood Will.

EDIBLE GRACE

I'm pushing a cart down the And/Or aisle of Stoner's Mind Department Store and discover just what I need—miscellaneous warnings and advice in bulk. I scoop them into a brown paper bag. Instantly they became a Quandary. My twin, who has come along, questions this, which is her right and which she always does, so we proceed to the front which could also be the back. "How do we know a fact is not also a fiction, a poem not also a prayer?" We ask the Fact Checker, who moonlights at Salvador Dali's Deli—famous for the world's tiniest sandwich so small it could fit in a matchbox, but so dense no one can lift it. So, this leaves us with our Quandary, a collective noun undefined.

An octopus, by the way, has three hearts and eight tentacles with minds of their own. Imagine the poetry an octopus could write, multiplied by eight. Imagine the pencils alone, ha! Our Fact Checker rings us up and asks, "Would you like a receipt?" We assure them we've had nothing to drink, and we're pretty sure it's a fact.

At the Care Facility, I visit a diminishing friend and am mistaken for a patient. In a heartbeat, I sign out at the front desk and go for a bike ride in the breezy afternoon under a sky so blue just to prove I'm not. The jury's still out. So I write this poem and pray.

My twin fits her shadow exactly into mine, and for a moment, we are one—with eight tentacles but only two hearts—and the need to dissect fact from fiction, poem from prayer means less than a tiny sandwich we can't eat. When in doubt, we make cookie dough and lick the beaters. Is any art more beautiful than chocolate chip cookies baking in an oven, any truth greater than that sweet aroma filling the house? Edible grace, our ticket to the sun.

RESUME FOR A GURU

I'm applying for the job of guru you advertised on Craigslist. My name is Barbed Wire, barbed wire having been the first thing my mother saw upon opening her eyes following my birth under the bushes on the dairy farm. I live up to my name – thin, strong, intermittently sharp. Few cross me. Barbs speak louder than words. Enormous mammals in fact keep their distance. Few dare attempt to trespass or escape. I'm a keeper of herds. A catcher of roving tumble-weeds. Artists make ironic statements with my strands. I lead a simple life. Am light on this earth. Solid posts being my only attachments. You see me along the road, atop a fence, on ranches and prisons, galvanized and strong, classic and secure, capable of containing man, beast, & belief.

GLASS MAN

She hires him to garden, skinny dips in the pool while he prunes. Invites him in. The water, cool on his skin. Her kids are scattered worldwide. Husband died poolside. She cackles. Backstrokes to the edge; he follows underwater. They go inside. Her friends visit. He washes their cars. Bartends. Pretends side eyes amuse him. Through streaky windows, he sees Mt. Tam, where once he was a grower. Rubs clean the indoor Ficus leaves. Hands go chamois soft. Her window washer arrives with suitcase. Tosses truck key, says, *Polish the hitch*. She beckons Glass Man upstairs, voice prehistoric like the heron who mistook the pool for a pond.

LANGUAGE OF LINES

I draw my clothes and wear them for a day.

Today a denim jacket, gardener's pants, and a green beret. If this is my superhero power, I won't be saving the world anytime soon, but I will be happily dressed.

Spiderman was bitten by a spider, and so his new life began.
I came from a typo myself, careless fingers on a keyboard.
Some origin story.

I am not a fashionista. I'm not even an artist. But the clothes I draw, simple as they are, come off the page.

I draw a closet for my drawn clothes but forget the key. I draw a car, but it has no gas, so I draw a bike, but alas, two flats.

Okay. I draw me, stick figure with flippy hair and call myself Maine because ME is how you abbreviate it. I draw you, but you can't come out to play.

I draw fringed bell bottoms and a shirt with pockets everywhere. In one pocket, I find a fortune: *Good news will arrive in the mail.*

I draw a smile. I draw a mailbox, only it looks more like a box on a stick. And guess what, there's a kitten inside—two, an orange tabby and a velvety black and white. And I

didn't draw them. They love the box and love to play. They're hungry, and I draw some food. They take to the kibble that looks maybe like Cocoa Krispies, a weakness of mine.

I draw a ladder down from the box, but they just leap and land on the grass, and I draw and draw one grass blade ahead as they tumble and rumble, crouch, and stare at gulls I draw overhead.

I think about what they need. Cats are a big responsibility. I draw a thought. I draw myself having a thought. I draw an ocean with a wide beach, a hillside with tall trees, a benevolent sun, boats at sea on the horizon.

I draw a new you. I draw a new me. I draw a poem with no letters about us. I draw a word bath on a page with no lines; I draw a cup of coffee and sip while I soak.

The cats walk along the edge of the tub, rascals both. I advise against hopping in, but you can no more control a cat than a hand across a blank page with a pen, staying one stroke, one line, one dot ahead of relentless imaginings, drawings, lines, and sentences, the conduits of the soul, the line, which Klee said is just a dot that went for a walk.

I draw a walking stick, a path through the trees to places I haven't drawn yet, primitive, but my drawing is getting better and so are my dreams, that is to say, they allow themselves to be remembered now, though they're still too shy to sit for a drawing and bare all while others scrutinize, assess, and express opinions which absolutely defy drawing and how could I ever trust, believe in, or care to hang out with that which can't be drawn, itself a conclusion.

The cats curl up together, magnificent tails at rest.

I draw myself a couch, a pillow, and float on a cloud. I can't pretend to draw a nap, so I draw myself looking up beyond clouds to the past, listening to the crash of gravitational waves on distant shores, gazing at the future, my feet pointing up, my arms hanging down, fingers at rest. Then I draw a question mark, pleased with the shape delighted by the wonder it conjures.

I see clouds drawn by others. I see light. I see dark. I see color. I draw a place to land. In a draw, of course, protected from raging storms which I do not draw.

I draw cutoffs and sandals. I draw a cotton shirt.

I draw my stick arms waving hello. I draw.

Will you draw back, hello?

EVAN'S ESSENCE

I visited my friend Evan at the V.A., found him in bed, smiling, wearing baggy flannels. Asked how he was doing.

"Oh, fine," he said, like it was last year, or five years ago, or fifteen or twenty.

I poured him a glass of water, noticed his left hand was gone. We played checkers until he started yawning. I promised to return.

The next day he was still in flannels, but these were blue, and red checked, soft and comfy—just like smilin' Ev. His big brown eyes were even bigger behind thick glasses he now wore. His feet were gone, kept it to myself.

We played checkers, talked baseball. Would the Giants repeat as champs, this being an odd year? Superstitious like any old player, Ev shrugged, grinned his Cheshire grin and drifted off.

I couldn't get to the VA for three days. When I entered his room Evan smiled, gone from the chest down now, covers pulled up around his neck. We skipped checkers and baseball, he asked about the kids—typical Evan. He was doing this his way.

Didn't stop me from crying.

"Don't be sad, Kenny. You're seeing the best of me. There's no time to complain about Lincecum's curveball or worry about who owes who money," which made me wonder whether I'd repaid him that 5-spot when we went to see On Any Sunday in 8th grade.

We talked motorcycles. I reminded him how he'd had his helmet and gloves before he had his first bike.

Evan chuckled. "Always wanted to be ready."

Saturday evening his nurse Shangri-La nodded gently and showed me to his room. I stared at rumpled covers, saw his smile on the pillow below those glasses. His lips moved. I edged closer, wondering if he was confessing his love for Shangri-La or admitting that he'd finished my stool in woodshop, helping me graduate on time, or perhaps he was imparting a universal secret, being the most agile spiritual explorer I ever knew . . . and I think he whispered, "Love's the current upon which we ride."

His smile faded. Evan vanished. And his essence filled the room.

The monitor flashed. Shangri-La threw back the curtains. Outside, the wind blew. Slender palms bent back and forth as if waving goodbye. A shooting star arced a silver trail against the satin sky. Somewhere, a baby beckoned.

Shangri-La slipped away to complete her rounds.

THE TRAP

You awake to the sound of screeching and scratching and clawing and what sounds like an unruly gang just outside your bedroom window at 3 am. You slip on your sweats, grab a flashlight and the .22 and go into your backyard. Near the pond, a circle of raccoons surrounds the *Have A Heart* trap that you set for whatever's been eating the lily pads and koi near the meditation bench. You figured it was maybe an opossum, skunk, or rat. You were wrong. You have an abiding hatred for raccoons—juvenile delinquents with claws who know how to open trash cans and cat doors, wreak havoc in the garden, and eat your very expensive prized koi - including Lazarus, your favorite who won't be coming back.

The circle of critters surrounding their trapped comrade scatters and retreats to the hedges of rhododendrons and azaleas, and you see the bright eyes of the trapped raccoon staring back at you in the early morning moonlight.

You know what you are going to do before you do it.

You know it goes against your Buddhist teachings.

You know it's nothing you can share with Joanie - in whose doghouse you've already taken up long-term residence, which happens to be the guest room in the dark corner of the house with the patchouli scent of her sister who won't be visiting again anytime soon still lingering, within earshot of said pond.

You set the iPhone timer for four minutes and hold the trap underwater. The morning goes silent, except for the garbage truck whose reverse beeping you can hear from blocks away. The animals watch you from the fence, eyes red in the dark.

You watch back. Defiant. This is your yard. Not theirs. And this little bastard, if he lived a mindful life, might get lucky and come back as someone's pet cat, or maybe a guide dog, or a dolphin in the sea. Real evolution. Suburban raccoons lead a wretched existence. Fish out of water living in these neighborhoods.

You look grimly at the submerged trap, thinking - bad pun, wondering if the surviving koi are swimming past the dead predator now, doing victory laps below the surface.

Finally, the harp music sounds, and you turn the timer off with your thumb and pull up the trap. It's heavier than expected. Water cascades out, and you decide not to look inside. You decide you don't want this trap. You don't want to ever do this again. Even though what you did was right. You're sure of it. Conflicted. But sure, yeah. The amount of money you save in replacement koi and lily pads alone will buy you ten more traps if it comes to that. You throw the whole mess into a triple-wrapped hefty bag and walk like a Demon Santa through the dark neighborhood in your black sweats, past Volvos and lawn sprinklers and garden art from Sunset Magazine -—leaving the .22 near the meditation bench - that could be awkward if you were stopped. You see the garbage truck ahead. And when the garbage man crosses the street for two cans, you heave the hefty bag into the yawning opening of the big noisy truck and walk away.

All the next day, you see signs. The radio plays Rocky Raccoon. Frances, the barista at the *Corner Cap*, moans that she has raccoon eyes. You google raccoon. Pictures of cute little bandits, startlingly human, gaze back at you.

 Over coffee, you tell Syd about it. He's quiet. Doesn't finish his croissant.

 That evening he cancels the meditation session you both always have on Thursdays. The next day he cancels coffee.

 You think of that raccoon. You sit by the pond and meditate. The .22 sits on the rock stupa you made from Russian River Stone. A balancing act. Rusty garden art. You think life isn't always so simple and clear. Especially in the heat of the moment. What heat? It was three in the morning. It was, in fact, chilly. Cold-blooded.

 You realize what you are capable of. A strange awakening. Unwanted enlightenment. Your friend Syd has realized this, too, apparently.

 The way you both realized it about AJ when he confessed his ongoing affair with the Swiss au pair and his wife Lilly never had a clue. Awkward because Lilly was a friend.

 After that, AJ had been uninvited to meditation.

 Silently voted off Zazen Island.

 We learn what we are capable of.

 We learn what others can do, exceeding our expectations.

 We learn how the person in front of us whom we sit zazen with, whom we share coffee with, has secrets.

You wonder how to reconcile all of this. You wonder about the word reconcile itself. How it's close in sound to raccoon. Reconcile Raccoon. Raccoonciliation.

An orange koi named Benji surfaces. Peers at you and disappears into the murky depths of the pond you haven't cleaned for weeks now.

The raccoons have not returned.

You look to the house. A curtain falls in the window of Joanie's room.

Since when did you start calling it Joanie's room?

And since when did you call yourself a Buddhist?

And Syd, your best friend?

You reach for your iPhone. See that the timer is still set on four minutes.

Hit Contacts.

Take a deep breath, hold, exhale: 1-2-3-4-5.

Press AJ.

DOG PARK 101

I'm at the dog park with Mumph, and he's at it again. Part Boxer, part Ridgeback, part Great Dane—pure scoundrel. Checking my emails at the picnic table, I hear the pack of dogs thunder by, and of course, I know whom they're chasing. It's a hump or be humped world for Mumph, and once again, he went one hump too far, this time with a German Shepard, a Pit, a Rott, and a Shiatsu on his tail, along with an owner in a trench coat and black glasses bringing up the rear.

We're running out of dog parks. The apartment complex has no yard, and Mumph needs to get out. Needs to run. And clearly needs to hump, though he was fixed at the pound before I adopted. Or he adopted.

Life was in full-swing-tilt before he came along.

The pack swings back my way again. Mumph is still in front, but now the enraged owner of a labradoodle with a trailing streak of red hair is gaining on him. I tap my iPhone closed and make my way to the dog park gate where all the chewed-up tennis balls come to rest, next to the murky water trough & plastic clean-up bags. I snap my fingers as Mumph sails past, catching his eye—his tongue now starting to hang, and for a moment I allow myself to admire his form, his beautiful muscular build, his stride, his speed, even if he is a knucklehead and loves to piss off the crowd. We've all known someone like that, I'm sure. But how many of them have a gatekeeper to bail them out?

So I stand outside the gate and hold it open, and here they come—the Shepard, Rott, labradoodle owner, and now a six-toed Tabby who looks a little large to be a pet. Mumph is losing ground and makes it through the entrance by a nose—just ahead of the long curvy nails of labradoodle mom. I slam the gate closed, and we make it to the hatchback in time to roll up the windows—quickly fogged —lock the doors, and leave the chaos behind.

Humph, I say, as if it were a typo, when are we gonna learn bro? When?

We pass the pound on the way home. Mumph's head hangs out the window, taking in the breeze. I wonder if he has memories of his previous life, if he has any idea how much he means to me, despite the difficulties, not to mention cleaning deposits he's cost me.

But he's family. Which doesn't always mean much, of course. There's a Trump-loving brother I don't talk to and the whole Eastern Seaboard of relatives who don't send me Christmas cards. But yeah.

Maybe dog parks just aren't our cup of chai. I hang a left onto Highway 1 and head to the coast for a little beach I know called Scoundrel's Last Refuge, Mumph now fast asleep on a giant flattened bean bag that is both my trunk and backseat. And sometimes my bed.

AFFORDABLE SHAKESPEARE

He worked at the Book Depot & Cafe. She cleaned houses on the
hill. They were in love and not yet married, not even talking about
it. At night they cleaned The Depot. He ate leftover muffins from
the café side, and they read all the books they wanted, careful not to
leave crumbs on the pages. He loved thin stories. She loved Dickens.
At home in their ground-floor flat, he wrote about the war he'd
left behind in Guatemala. She studied for nursing school. They fell
asleep listening to the tapping typewriters of the writers upstairs. He
opened The Depot at dawn. By noon, Don Carpenter held court at
his favorite table. 'Sure,' the old author would kindly say, 'send your
work to my agent.' It was Paris for him, young love for them. On
Sundays, they drank coffee in iron chairs atop the barbershop and
watched the crowds walking the leafy streets. They were 22 and they
owned that town.

MEASURE

You measure the room with the Stanley tape, careful of your fingers when the metal strip retracts. You like the high-speed sound it makes disappearing into the case. 5'3" x 5'9". You do the math. Doesn't look good. This room was once a closet, this house a summer cabin for San Franciscans seeking sunshine in July. Now it's going to be a second bedroom in a house for five: you, Felicia, two strays, and a baby well on the way.

The crib is 6 feet long. A gift from Felicia's dad, who didn't ask for dimensions, just bought it on Amazon, had it delivered. Unassembled. The crib is in pieces on the kitchen floor, instructions spread across the table covering the fruit bowl. Felicia's on bed rest in the master bedroom, itself barely six feet long—were people shorter back then?—resting with the two strays and baby in utero, unaware of this math problem, and depending on you to figure things out. You practice a deep Lamaze breath, refold the instructions—a crisp map for a journey you're not sure you're built for—and you squeeze into the cozy double bed, leaving a tiny space between you and Felicia where a baby-sized pillow now fits.

LESSON 3: HOW TO GET PICKED

Educated at the half court on Caledonia you majored in position, minored in hustle, and learned to love the no-look pass. When the big man backed you down in the low post you learned to step aside and pull the chair, hands in the air, and learned never to take credit for gravity. That day sweet-shooting Charley said that with four just like you he'd take on all comers, you arrived. Thirty-five years later, you pass a limping ghost in the frozen food aisle at Golden Gate Market and you both smile, remembering those asphalt Saturdays under the rusty rim with no net.

WHAT DARWIN FAILED TO MENTION

My evolution began when a novice magician at an open mic panicked while pulling me out of the hat and fled the stage. Partially complete, I climbed out myself and finished the show. With these ears of a rabbit, this body of a man, I've been called Rabbit Man, Hare Freakma, Flopsy, Mopsy, Cottontail, and Peter. Once someone shouted, "Hey, Mr. McGregor's coming," as if to scare me.

Dude, I'm fucking made of porcelain. The only thing I'm scared of is gravity. I steer clear of high shelves and stupid questions.

People love to stare at what appalls them. They can't look

away. Can't pocket the iPhone. So they pay. Monetize your abomina-
tions. What Darwin failed to mention is that at times we make our
own breaks. The guilt bone is the weakest link in human anatomy.
Churches strike gold with it. Con artists make bank.

I met Giraffe Man once, didn't envy him. Sparrow Woman.
Calico Kid. Scandal has a shelf life. I'm all ears. For a price, I'll tell
you what you want to know.

People ask if I like to hop. Chew on a carrot. Fuck, of course.
One kid wanted to rub my foot for luck. As if I'm a figment with
no feelings. Not once have I been asked what it's like to be frozen in
evolution, caught between species. Once, an old man with a burro
nose inquired about intimacy in a soft bray. Would Darwin be
surprised by his origin story? Funny you should ask. Funny I could
answer. It'll cost you 20.

For the record, Halloween's my favorite holiday. I win Best Costume
every year. Unless Giraffe Man shows up in his fedora. Or Crow Girl,
who does this little trick with Jack Daniels. For my money, props
call for an asterisk in the win column. You could say I'm a purist. You
wouldn't be wrong.

People wanna know if I got stuck evolving from human to
rabbit or hare, or rabbit or hare to human. A zebra is black with white
stripes, but I'm not gonna tell 'em that. I tell 'em, good question.
PayPal or Venmo work for me.

No, I've never seen Lochness Monster. You think we're all
alike? Hang out at the same water cooler? I may have seen BigFoot
once at an Evolution Anonymous Meeting, smoking in back. After
the serenity prayer, he vanished. So did the donuts. Damn cross
addictions. I was starved. But it could've been Chewbacca's son. I
hear he's grown some.

I never believed in all 12 steps, when seven or eight would do. I slow down for no one. We know how that ends.

Once, I dated the poet Tigressa, there are a lot of words. She started reading me her poems, no time limit. I started charging by the syllable.

My sponsor's Owl Lady. She doesn't say much. But those unblinking eyes of hers will unnerve you if you stray. Okay, I've got some amends to make.

I do like to swim and have a healthy respect for sharks, who get a bad rap. Dolphins are the real badasses of the sea. If you want someone out of the gene pool, don't let Flipper's smile fool you. Heard him spill his guts at a meeting. Well, someone's guts.

That's why they call our meetings anonymous.

Why I use a stage name, Magician. These days I have a little side hustle as a life coach, and still work a few birthdays, bar mitzvahs, and the occasional bachelorette party.

Seriously, if I were you and you were me, I wouldn't believe a word of it. Belief has nothing to do with truth anyway. Belief is a scandal with no shelf life. That's some hybrid power shit. Truth requires no faith. No facts. No opinions—which, by the way, Taoists hold in tiny regard.

So, what is truth, you ask?

That'll cost you another 20.

That's the truth.

JANE

It started with a fake name at Starbucks.

"Harry," I told the barista, Destiny.

"Gary?" she asked.

"No. Harry." I watched her write H-A-I-R-Y on the paper cup with a Sharpie.

Harry was an old man's name now, a name that belonged to a different generation, like Walter or George or Dick. Wait. Was I old now? AND hairy??

I paid for my double decaf, answering my own question as usual without any help.

All that day I used fake names. At the dry cleaner's I was Johan. At the dog park with my sister's corgi, I was Rolf. On a blind date that night, I became Kam. "With a K," I said making that part up on the fly to the woman, Jane. Or was it Frieda?

Most people stretch the truth about income, health benefits, age. For me, it was all about the name. After the second scotch, I fessed up. Jane looked at me kind of funny and I could see in her dark eyes there was no going back—not to the truth, not to the first hug, and not to her place, or mine.

Pity. I was into her. A poet. Who liked Black Label. Wore high boots. Named Jane.

She asked for our check before dessert from the waiter, Paulo. Pulled out cash for a little over half the amount. I could see she liked to tip after tax.

"I'd like to call you again," I said "Such a good time. What's your last name, Jane?"

She closed her small black purse. Flashed a fading smile. "Doe."

THE MOST SHOPLIFTED POET IN AMERICA

"Would Bukowski be in poetry?" I ask the young man who is reading behind the counter. I'd already gone to the poetry section and perused the 'B's with no luck.

The young man smiles. "We keep Bukowski behind the counter here."

"Why is that?"

"He's the most shoplifted poet in America."

Once in a Venice Beach bookstore, I'd gone to the "B's" and found the same thing.

The clerk invited me behind the counter, and I discovered a treasure trove of Bukowski titles I'd never seen. Above Bukowski was

John Fante, also on the endangered list. Interesting because Fante was not well known, but Bukowski admired him, was a friend. Did that mean the book thieves were actually reading Bukowski and then Fante to see what Buk saw? Feel what he felt?

Who else? I wanted to know.

"Murakami," said the clerk.

"Hmm . . . what about Carver?"

"No, Carver's safe."

"Well, wait till the Murakami shoplifters find out how much he liked Raymond Carver. Those books will fly off the shelves."

The clerk grinned. There was a time I had to stop reading Buk. Rejection will do that to you. A magazine editor had declined a piece of mine and said I had to quit sleeping with Bukowski under my pillow. I doubt he ever stole a Bukowski. I doubt he ever stole anything.

I paid for a copy of *Factotum*, shook the young clerk's hand. He was a screenwriter, taking a couple of years off grad school at UCLA. MFA? Yeah.

Years ago, I had worked in a bookstore and was pleased to see people were still interested. It restored my faith, I told him. He nodded and turned to the register to make change.

I slipped a copy of *What We Talk About When We Talk About Love* into my large leather coat.

Ray deserved that.

THINGS HAVE A WAY OF DISAPPEARING AROUND HERE

We're messy, we know. Orderliness is the enemy   ity.
Our spice rack is arranged intuitively. Oregano &
Basil = pasta sauce, Pepper & Sage = steak, Tylenol & Vodka =

But the story we wrote on a pad of white paper cannot be
found.

And our checkbook's turned invisible. And that plastic cap
that covers the blade on the apple peeler is also missing. Meanwhile,
apples cover the yard, freshly fermented, baked by the sun.

When they drop and hit the ground we always look up.
Yellow, green, and red – unlike that missing story we wrote in
bed, unread, or the clear plastic blade-covering cap that we just saw
this morning –

"Well it didn't just grow legs and walk away now did it?"

On the table, we move around boxes of family photos to be filed, the dog's prednisone and the cat's insulin, along with a broken cookie jar waiting to be glued, a mason jar of eco-sustainable one-syllable words, and a compost bin of clichés ready to be ⬡ _imagine_ ed.

A pattern emerges. Not exactly symmetrical or hard-edged, we grant - none>the>less classical abstract expressionism, with a hint of Absurd Clarity: "The plastic cap writes checks that the story can't cash,"

which absolutely flies in the face of all that mother taught us.

Clearing a space

           on the counter, we uncover a plot to build a shower-powered bathtub porsche. This idea entices us. Not as much as the slice of fudge cake we also uncover
The However Cake.

The plan is dated 1959. Below:
In time, no one exactly remembers.

We concur. Which is why we stick to fiction, although we always got A's in history.

LOVERS OF A
BYGONE ERA

It was never about camping, or hiking, or climbing to the top of a peak, or bird watching, or getting back to nature, or cowboy coffee over a campfire in the morning, or making love in a tent, or sharing a sleeping bag for two, or even one. You were scared of heights, and I was scared of you. Leaving. *Face your fears*, said your yoga teacher Zario.

A weekend retreat, though you refused to use that word. *Let's call it a weekend advance instead*, you said, and I—out of my league, unable to touch my toes, unable to empty my mind, unable to even breathe right, the one who farted while trying 'downward dog' in front of the class—went along.

The trail was precarious at best. Mountain goats would have been put to the test. On the climb up, I filled the silence with chatter. *Did you know goats have different accents depending on where they're from?*

Animal facts felt real to me. So did the chain handrail as I inched up the narrow ledge of straight-down mountain. *Dodo birds had wings but never flew*, I said, *only used them for balance like a tight-rope walker.* Wouldn't they be handy right about now, I laughed. Of course, Dodos became extinct. Bad ideas have a way of finding their way out of the gene pool, right?

You were focused, silent, tongue stuck out in concentration. I wore tennis shoes, you hiked barefoot. I thought of what we called waffle stompers in the '70s. It seemed a new day then—down jackets, gorp, and hiking boots with enormous textured soles. Now my Adidas felt inadequate as I trailed you, followed your footprints in the dirt. How could that not hurt? Granite and shell, mountain thorns. You were somewhere else.

Embracing pain, you did not feel it. Releasing fear, it let you go. Letting go of the chain freed you from all attachments...the PR job you despised, the condo with its dreaded homeowner's association (a cult of self-importance, you called it), and FEAR itself—fear of falling, fear of dying, fear of missing out, and fear of being alone with me, apparently.

I stood on the trail gripping the chain, unable to move forward, unable to go back. Iron links penetrated my palms. A shiver of altitude passed through me.

Flannery O'Connor made the papers as a six-year-old when she taught a chicken to walk backward. The longest flight of a chicken on record is 13 seconds. Thirteen seconds. I eased my grip, finger-tipped the chain, and stared at the side of the mountain.

An inch from my nose, an ant made its way over a rock and encountered another ant. *Ants bow to each other in greeting.* You were no longer there to hear that fact. See that act of wonder. Ants herd aphids and drink their sugary liquid; the only animals to farm other animals though it sounded more like slavery to me. As usual, I'm at my pithiest when no one's there to hear me, with no paper to write down deep thoughts.

Paralyzed in place, I marveled at the priceless, worthless million-dollar view below. Moa was the only known bird born without wings. Huge and friendly, they were easy prey, walking targets, extinct by the 1400s. Did Zario believe in extinction? Is that what happened if you couldn't touch your toes? Failed to execute Mountain Pose on a steep ledge? There was no advancing, no retreating. No growing wings. No forgetting the fact book you gave me for Valentine's Day, Animals of A Bygone Era.

Back in the '70s, Paul Simon said there were 50 ways to leave your lover. I said, let's make it 51, and let go.

WE DEVOURED BOOKS

beginning with covers. chapter by chapter, page by page until we got down to letters, the small bones of words which we consumed like the cooked sardines we ate in Portugal, heads and all. you said some were smiling. we drank cold beer and digested the honeymoon knowing someday words would be written, covers torn asunder, pages swallowed, words picked clean trying to glean what lay between the lines.

SATURDAY MORNING

The cats don't know it's Saturday. Pontiac hops on the bed and meows to be fed, standing in the empty place where Pearl used to sleep. I open one eye and get a fix on the clock: 5:23. Way too early for a weekend. I hold out a hand. Try to mollify with a stroke of his silky head. Pontiac keeps his distance.

Jade Blue the Siamese is having her way with the carpet. I roll over and close my ears. That's when Pontiac goes to Level 2 and starts licking my lobe. After four scratch pad licks, I'm back on my back and the big dude goes heavy, stepping onto my chest with all fours taking away any chance I have to breathe. He knows it. I know it. It's time.

Truth is Pontiac belonged to Pearl. She'd rescued him from an ex who had been ignoring the enormous, needy Tabby. Now I was part of the ex-line. Somehow Pontiac stayed behind. I get it. Pearl's a nomad who lives on cinnamon, coffee, and cigarettes, who loves pomegranates and cats-in-need, who looks younger and more waifish by the day, with a turquoise voice that holds every cafe captive when she takes her turn at the mic.

I speak from experience.

I stagger to the kitchen and speak to Pontiac who purrs against my legs. Jade Blue waits by the window, content to let the big fella work. I open a fresh can of Fancy Feast. Pontiac meows. Rises on his back legs. Jade Blue joins the party.

"I know. I miss her, too." I set the open can on the counter and take a small pleasure in making them wait just a little while longer. Rascals.

And I put the coffee on.

WHEN THE LIGHTS COME ON

You go to Bali to write a book and do anything but. You want to tell the world about the fishermen's wives in Sri Lanka, made widows by the tsunami, whom the priest tells you about, introduces you to. They are Muslim, feel threatened, and keep to themselves. They welcome you slowly. They ask what your life is like as a nurse, a psychologist, a mother, a wife. You have come as a trauma worker, to do what you can. You ask what they need, how you can help. They say they need lights. At night. You nod, thinking they want to read, share stories, weave. At night, they say, village men enter their tents and rape them. The air leaves your chest. The world leaves you remote and horrified and spinning, and when you regain your upright balance you go to the village priest.

You arrange for lanterns and kerosene and the priest, a manic thin man on a motorcycle sees that they are delivered. On your last day in the country, he says there is something he wants to show you, and he takes you to the tents at the edge of the sea. At dusk, the lights come on. And you see the glowing rows, the brilliant light cast against the darkness and dangers that come out at night, and you are overcome.

So you go to Bali to write, a widow yourself now, and you do everything but. You fall in love. You swim daily. You get hit by a motorcycle, and it breaks you up. Badly.

You come home to your daughter's—a floating home where every day you rise and fall with the tide. Your brain floats in a pool of blood. Your head begins to heal. Your hair turns beautiful silver, more silver than you are old. The love of your life, gone. Your daughter goes to work each day. The coffee is strong. The light on the water moves in strange and gentle ways. You sit by the window in a chair with a cat, a journal, and a pen you don't own. You turn on the floor lamp. Smell kerosene.

HEADLONG

It was not sustainable. As if life itself had no shelf life. You knew
it could only end as a train wreck even when the tracks were clear
and the countryside rolled by. Porters were tipped and dismissed,
their services not needed. The sleeping car had everything—stocked
mini-fridge, mini bottles of Johnny Black, picture window, fold-out
bed, eyeshades, earmuffs, pillow mints, and Alexa, who was fluent in
Thelonius and Trane.

Three rolling days stretched endlessly ahead with Pirate Poet
in the dining car, stately women silently saying grace, a card trickster,
and Stingy Brim Brother with an unlit pipe.

Rolling away from the past you knew it couldn't last, a life in
robes, love in the afternoon, aware moments become memory, people
become objects they leave behind: denim shirt, felt hat, photograph,
a laugh, a final cigarette before dawn in a no-smoking car, windows
open, triangle of moonlight on the floor, towel tucked under the
door as if no one would know. No one but you. Until it was only you.
And the train. And the wall. Headlong.

TWO-PENNY TOUR

I wake up on this periodic table and recognize nothing. I memorized my times tables through 10 in the 3rd grade, every other class learned them through 12. Some things you never forget. The old cat always finds the litter box. My pen always finds words for the page. After mom died, I returned from the cemetery to find a crowd haggling over her stuff on the lawn. I can tell you what I'll take a nickel for. And what I won't.

FICTION, SUPPOSEDLY

1. Suppose

You discover in your 60th year that your father was a molester, had been molested himself. By his father.

Suppose you discover that your grandfather, whom you never knew, was not only a molester but most likely had been molested too.

By his adopted father.

Suppose you learn all this over conversation with your cousin whom you barely knew growing up, being 19 years older than you.

Suppose he asks you if your father had ever hurt you, as you sit at his kitchen table drinking coffee looking out over DC at the sunset-lit horizon through leafless trees. A city with all its history that you love so much.

2. The Belt

Suppose you tell your cousin about the two times your father took his belt to you, one for sure, but two you think. Leaving welts on your bare six-year-old legs, whippings you haven't thought of for 50 years, now a vivid 50-year memory. Well stored like preserves in the back of the pantry.

Those words canning/caning: practically cousins themselves...

But you can tell as he carefully, thoughtfully stirs his black coffee and watches you that belt whippings are not what he has in mind.

And you're wondering at that moment over coffee as a 60-year-old man, as a writer, as a teacher, as a father yourself looking back at your 6-year-old, 7-year-old self, what kind of person does that to a kid? What kind of grownup takes a belt to a young child's bare legs?

Suppose you're about to find out as your cousin, 6 years younger than your father, tells you that your father molested him, and his sister, one summer when he stayed at their house... stayed, to get away from his own monster dad.

3. Gallo

Suppose you'd heard the stories about your dad living with them— but a far different version—how the kids in Española had mercilessly teased him about the name you both would share, calling him Gallo, rooster. One thing your dad could never stand was being embarrassed. Humiliated. Poor man's pride.

So, he'd left Española at 15, for the summer or so you'd been told, to live with relatives in California, to get away from the gang for a while, and when he returned home hoping for a fresh start, he began going by his middle name, a name you also share being a Jr., but despised.

Suppose you don't consider yourself a junior. They'd always called you Chip.

But you were no chip off the old block, were you? And if you were an apple, you fell and rolled far away from the tree. Fell and kept rolling.

Rolling still...

4. Lurking

You are 60 years old now, and suddenly your world is rocked, and everything you thought you knew, everyone you thought you loved, every poem you ever wrote, every story of him you ever put down had another side lurking in the shadows.

You call your one remaining sister. And ask her. No, she assures.

You exhale, and so you tell her what you've learned.

You both remember how your older sister spoke ominously of your father's brother, Uncle Herm, nothing specific but an unmistakable fear, hint of shudder to her tone that you both recall, pushing away from memory's table: a warning to never leave your kids. Alone. With Herm. So close to Harm.

You learn all this in what you hope is the 3rd quarter of your life... though 63 is the expiration date of those in your family who went before you.

The common denominator in your genes.

And now, what are you supposed to do with this? Your father, your mother, your older sis...long gone.

5. Craft

Your cousin, 81, is now writing a novel. His first. You offer to help. Because it's what you do. Because you like your cousin. Because you want to help.

Because you feel helpless and can only fall back on what you do best, craft.

Penance? Is that what this is, you wonder, for despicable actions your dead father committed as a teen? So you read. And it's a story about a distant grandfather five generations back who joins a religious cult led by a charismatic, dogma-filled snake oil salesman, a fake miracle man who collects wives, who attracts crowds, who gathers allies to collaborate in lethal charades. Whose followers ignore the outrageous, the obscene, the barbarous acts of this leader.

Because they want to believe.

And so they do.

He becomes their portal to God, to pleasure and bliss. No matter what he does.

Because he's the one they've been waiting for. The art of the deal with the devil. You read vivid, harsh realistic rape scenes— raping of women, raping of young boys at revivals in the dark.

You try to edit for grammar. Sentence construction. Tense changes. Verb agreement. Point of view. Editing, never your strong suit. Editing, tolerated as necessary carpentry. Editing, safe now. Safe as the side of the pool in the deep end where you never swam.

Suppose all you can imagine, as you read these evocative horrible scenes, is your father doing this to your cousin and his sister. And having it done to him.

And his father before him...

Grammar seems beside the point. Same with point of view. Verb agreement. Spelling. Past tense becomes the story of your life.

You wonder about your own DNA. What shadows did you inherit?

What horrible tendencies course through your blood?

When you're done reading your cousin's story, all you can say is: Powerful. Moving. Brilliant. An extraordinary novel. First novel, or otherwise.

It came from somewhere deep.

Because it's true. And thank you. And...I am so sorry. So so sorry. Because that, too, is true.

6. Pearl

You wonder how a family doesn't talk about this...as if secrets untold meant they did not happen. You've heard it happens in many families. But you think, we're not many families. This is/was my family. The way a doctor might say you have a rare disease. The way nothing seems rare when it happens to you.

You wonder what you are supposed to do with all of this, knowing it's all true, especially the fiction. Once in class, the question of truth arose when a new writer said she never wrote fiction because she didn't like to lie. And you quoted Fellini: "All art is autobiographical; the pearl is the oyster's autobiography."

You wonder, you wonder, you wonder. As you write, you

wonder.

As you talk with your cousin who has forgiven your father, you wonder.

You realize it's all you can do—wonder—because fiction has taught you how to navigate with uncertainty, surprise, and disbelief on the page as you move forward with your clock-ticking life and this new knowledge.

As you put the pictures of your father away, you wonder about the abuse he suffered as a boy, you wonder what kind of people do this to others. And you wonder what kind of people rise up and stop the cycle, circle, spiral, horror, and pain.

7. The Gift

Watching a sunset 3,000 miles from home, majestic colors of a vanishing sky, you think of the distance craft allows from your history, the chance to create something new from the ashes and ruins and monstrosities of the past, changing the arc, altering the endings of stories still in progress, finding new places to land.

But what kind of people can forgive, how is it even possible, you wonder, as you quietly sip coffee across the kitchen table from your cousin, new old friends, alone with your thoughts, your shared history, your lessons lived and learned.

And at last, you know.

POEM REPAIRS

The scaffolding around the house never comes down. Permanent fixture. Part of the furniture. Apparently, there's no end to repairs. Last year's leak over the stairs moved to the ceiling above the dining room, leaving deco-goth stripes running down the walls. Shingles above the front door were no sooner replaced when the awning out back eloped with a 40-knot wind. Life in the fast lane. Always work to be done.

At some point, life becomes maintenance; writing a poem an adjustment, a small remodel where feelings and perceptions dwell. No work to be done by licensed contractors. No permits and nothing subbed out. It's a do-it-yourself daily project. Though you do draw the line at tarps. Like blue-tarp-Buddha on the housepainter's roof, tarp flapping in the wind, concrete sculpture inscrutable, calm as cement. Pretty soon, you can't say when; it's one of those things that just happens; you get used to it. We're hard-wired evolutionaries.

You come to see scaffolding as part of the architecture. The neighbor's tabby comes to see it as a catwalk. At Christmas, you string it with lights. Housepainter's blue- tarp-Buddha gets a Santa's hat. You swear it cracks a smile though that may be concrete aging. Like so much of life, like anything really, it depends on how you look at it, how you brick and mortar the words as proof to catch up with a reality you like. Words as scaffolding to buttress the wall of opinion, drywall of belief.

So far, last year's repairs over the piano are holding. Like a pantry stocked with canned goods—chowder and minestrone, baked beans and black olives (who the hell bought the tuna, you glance at your cat), you feel ready for dry rot and wind, rain, and leaky pipes.

Pestilence and plague.
Ignorance and arrogance.
Rejection and acceptance.

Future repairs of any and all nature destined to appear in your forecast. Scaffolding grows on you. Grows on the house. Form follows function you tell yourself, and soon it is true. True, it's not how you drew it up, but neither is the Ducati in the living room. Neither is this poem. Cats are grateful for the scaffolding that never comes down, and neighbors eventually don't care. Daily you go about the pages of your life, making an honest living doing small poem repairs, like a fisherman who mends their net before setting out each morning to see what they will find.

TOMATO

In search of the perfect tomato, Lou hits the Farmer's Market on Sunday. The heirlooms are extravagant. One purplish-green monstrosity is on the grotesque side. He examines it closely, pulls back, feels the Farmer staring—and realizes the old guy resembles his tomato the way people sometimes resemble their dogs.

"How much for one?" Lou hopes for expensive, it'll be easy to say no. He remembers the cherry tomatoes his mother grew and ate from the vine, tossing one to the big German Shepard Francis, who politely swallowed it and waited for another.

"One dollar," says the Farmer.

Not wanting to offend, or appear miserly, Lou forks over a buck and takes the tomato home, thinking grilled cheese and tomato sandwich. But when he slices the heirloom, he forgets all about the sandwich and the Farmer and how the tomato looked. In one exquisite bite, Lou savors the taste of summer—this summer and all the summers of his past.

A CERTAIN STAR

They've come back a year after selling their mother's houseboat to us, Evan and Maryanne, visiting from the east coast, gazing at the changes, not so many, that we've made. But I forget the changes they see are not cosmetic—are drastic in their minds—I see it in their faces. Adele's bookcases are gone. Her Danish table is not here. Her art, some of which is hanging in their own house now, or in storage perhaps, has been replaced by ours.

I remember being unable to let go of anything for the longest time after my mother died, and then finally, in one of my addition-by-subtraction moods, I began to toss out stuff—old address books, cabbage patch dolls that never did become valuable, government pens . . . and being horrified after throwing out mom's driver's license when I saw her face peering up at me through the trash.

We're in the living room now, sipping water from blue glasses. High tide. Evan, his wife Maryanne, and I are floating on this sunny day. Light reflects off moving water. Colors of the houseboats across the channel create moving shapes that capture the moment and hold us in awe. Adele stories flow. She was sharp until the end, with a perfectly coiffed silver bob. Funny but flinty, as her son describes. Once, they gave her a small pillow with *Brown University* embroidered on it. It's where they'd all gone to school for generations.

She removed her readers, "Why did you give me this? I don't need it," and gave it back.

Living on a boat will do that. Nothing extra, only what you need, since living on the water, you already have everything. The night before she died, Adele told her visiting son how much she loved this houseboat. She was at the end of her life, though no one, except perhaps Adele, knew the last page would be written that night.

Fiona and I had lived next door for three years. Sometimes Adele joined our circle of writers. I mention the time that I told Adele about my writing class on addiction called Hooked. With a wry grin, she'd said, "For me, it's Chapstick, but I can quit anytime."

As we sit now in the afternoon listening to the creaks of the beams, the groans of the ramp, Evan's eyes rest on our bookcase. He and his brother had hastily gone through their mother's things, taking what they wanted to keep and leaving behind many of her possessions, including shelves of books, which I assured them was fine. Being from out of town, and needing to get back to their jobs, their lives, I'd offered to handle the rest. So when Fiona and I closed escrow and moved in, we sorted through stacks and stacks of books, keeping a few, donating boxes to the library.

Evan spies the spine of James Thurber's *Carnival*. "Was that mom's?"

I can't be sure. Fiona had inherited old books from her family, and I'm not certain if that Thurber had been Adele's or not.

"I remember growing up with that book," he says.

For a moment, it looks like he wants to get up from the chair, but he remains.

"Would you like to take the book?" I ask.

"Really? Why, yes. Yes, I would, very much. Thank you."

He glances at Maryanne. Something passes between them. "Oh, well, maybe not."

I'm relieved, not knowing whether the book had been a treasure passed down on Fiona's side, wondering if I was giving away something that wasn't mine to give but also inexplicably feeling a little possessive myself.

Looking at his face—longing, wistful and bittersweet, I can't help myself. "Are you sure?"

"Yes, I'm sure." Rising from the chair, Evan goes to the sink, rinses his glass of water, and prepares to leave.

Adele had carefully typed and taped notes to the walls around the houseboat for the short-term tenants she would rent to when she traveled: *Sometimes water leaks from this shower door. Just place the bathmat up against the door to keep the floor dry; Don't flush tampons down the toilet; Never flush or run water if the power goes out."* We left them up because when I read them, I can hear her voice. I watch as Evan reads the one over the sink, *Please don't use abrasive cleansers on countertops, cupboards, or stove.* He grins. Adele's grin.

Evan and Maryanne are gracious. They thank me for allowing them to drop by. We promise to get together again. I assure them the portal will always be open.

As they walk down the dock, I go back and find Thurber's *Carnival*, hoping to see a name written inside. There is none. The binding is fragile; the pages yellowed and textured, of good, thick paper. But delicate. The kind they don't make books out of anymore. Thurber's drawings and stories are magical. I open to *The Moth and*

Star. It begins with an earnest young moth telling his mother he has set his heart upon a certain star, and she suggests he set his sights upon a certain lamppost instead.

I carry the book out to the dock to see if Evan and Maryanne are still in sight. Perhaps they've lingered to gaze at Mt. Tam or to soak up the fading afternoon light in the dock's weathered grey Adirondack chairs.

But they're gone. I go back inside and promote Thurber's *Carnival* from the bookcase to the tippy stack by the chair where I sit every morning with coffee and one or two cats and begin each day with a story or poem, thinking of my own mother, my own certain star.

SHORT WALK ON A LONG PIER

Floating in the shadows of the Ferry where a famous master once zenned, lived a sippy monk on a tippy barge called The China Sea. Each morning he walked the planks with a satisfied stride, then untied koans of kelpy line until noon.

At lunch, he played chess with the seagulls on a skiff, and when high tide arrived, he paddled to the No Name for beer and read Li Po until 2.

No books were written about him. No one came to his door. But his elegant wisdom glittered like sea glass on the ocean floor. Lifting a conch shell to his ear, he heard the whisper of the universe. Placing the shell to his lips, he answered its call.

LIGHT EATER

Meg sat at a small table overlooking the garden, morning light streaming in through the window. I poured two cups and watched the cat crouching in bushes below the birdfeeder where random seeds had fallen. Sunlight illuminated the side of Meg's face, and strands of silver glowed electric in her hair. She sat radiant, still, and serene, lips slightly parted. I placed a cup next to her tangerine slices and buttered toast. She hadn't touched a bite.

SOCIALE

Plastic Jesus doesn't begin to cover what Carrie has glued to her dash. Plastic Wonder Woman wields a lasso. Bob's Big Boy holds a juicy burger. Monique the chicken cocks her plastic head above an ancient cassette player and gold Oscar stands erect and poised. Each has a story to tell. Like Carrie.

She's found a parking place in front of Club Sociale. It's a red zone of course but she'll fight the ticket, claiming she's color blind and thought she had 20 minutes. That's about all I can take myself.

Carrie calls her '72 Volvo art wagon *Mona*. The years of dust and rust and mud and dried concrete only add to the patina. *How you gonna run something like that through a car wash*—the rear hatch is covered with decades of bumper stickers. One is from McGovern's failed run against Nixon, but 'ern' is all that remains. Art wagon *Mona* reminds me of an urn - an urn for plastic toys, ancient wrenches, and rusty saw blades glued to her doors and fenders, with a spoke-less wheel on the roof that spins in the wind when she rolls down the road.

Original hybrid.

That's pretty much Carrie. How she got her hands on a cellphone to text me, I'll never know. But here I am. Twenty years too late.

What we had was once diagnosed as love. How we lived was once called communal. Two-Acre Farm. Just outside the little town we called Sebtopia, A place I don't return to anymore.

You could call it curiosity.

You could call it obligation.

You could call it penance, perhaps.

Entering the dim club on a bright afternoon, seeing Carrie in her tie-dye cape and peasant blouse wearing amber beads, I'd call it something else.

Two men in 49er caps sit on either side of her laughing at something she said. Carrie cackles. A bartender dries a glass, looking bemused, Brand F tattooed down her bicep.

Carrie grins when I say, "Hey," and I see she's down to two teeth in front. Her eyes go straight to my hair— or where my hair used to reside, but she keeps any assessment to herself. Barbers always check out your hair when they greet you, the way Dentists check out your teeth when you smile. She used to cut my hair on a stool out under the trees.

I nod at the two 49er-faithful, who, if posture has anything to say, seem less friendly now. They stay on their stools tipping back Buds.

"Wanna get a table?" I ask her.

"Oh yeah. You never liked sitting at the bar."

I shrug. "Your call."

But she's already flowing towards a booth with a view of the street where a cop is writing out her ticket.

"Close the tab?" asks Brand E.

Not much has changed. I order an Anchor Steam and leave money on the bar to cover all the drinks.

"Headed to Morocco," Carrie tells me. "Taking possession of a schooner."

"Casablanca?"

"Some things are just meant to be," she says with that smile.

"Gonna sail her back?"

"Not in hurricane season." Carrie twirls the stir stick from her daiquiri.

"Good idea," I say.

Her dad was a merchant marine; she grew up on a tug in Sausalito. We'd built a bark in the barn on the farm with firm intentions to sail south, though plans had a way of blowing off course in those gusty days we called the youth of our adulthood.

I take a sip. Cold Anchor Steam feels good going down. "So, you gotta crew?"

"Gonna single hand. Wondering if I can leave *Mona* with you."

"I live in a flat in Bernal Heights." I shrug. "No place to park."

"When did you start doing that?" she says. "It's kinda cute."

"What. Renting?"

"No, this." She shrugs and rolls her eyes.

I grin, shrug back. "Don't own a car anymore. Don't want one. I use Uber, Lyft. Sometimes I rent a zip car."

She raises her eyebrows, now almost invisible.

"What about your two new friends at the bar? The bros whose drinks I just bought."

Carrie laughs with a heave of her shoulders, a wheeze from her chest. The miles have not been kind.

"How about Candace and Ray?"

"They're gone." She gazes out the window. The new citation flaps in the breeze under a wiper blade. A man in Bermuda shorts is taking a picture of a woman in capris posing in front of *Mona*, and I can't decide whether they are time warp tourists or hipsters who've lapped me in the cool department.

We sit at the small table listening to Johnny Hodges. Both of us gray. One of us thin. Neither of us anywhere but here.

"So, there's no schooner," she says.

"I figured."

"But I am single-handing. And where I'm going, I can't take *Mona*."

I nod. The two unfriendlies have left the Club and Brand E. is vaping out front. A crowd gathers near the art car, checking out the right rear ouija board window. One guy spins the spoke-less wheel on the roof as if it's roulette.

We both know what number it will land on.

I reach across the table, rest my hand next to Carrie's, her fingers covered in rings. The Navajo turquoise I recognize from our peace corps training in Gallup.

In a heartbeat, they say. It's over just like that.

This goodbye I do not want. Not because it'll be our last, at least in this life, but because of what I now must say. And so I do.

"Sure, love, leave the keys with me."

TRANSLATED FROM THE ORIGINAL

Anytime you translate, a little part of you goes into someone else's creation.

That's the way it is. It's like seeing faces in a plank of wood.
Your eye catches the eyes, the set of a mouth, the shape of a head in a knotty 2x6 laid by an erstwhile carpenter.
Sometimes you wish you didn't see faces.

You can't help it.
It's part of your shape,
the way you look at the world,
and the way the world looks at you.

You find the Original Portable Tungesa Dictionary in Darko's Antiques on Main, the place that's never open, but is today, and though you don't speak Tungesa, and even your spellcheck wants to auto-correct it into something that trades more in its orbit, you have to have this book. You are the only one inside the store. A basket near the register sports a note: *Please leave a contribution, we're trying out the honor system today.*

And you think, it'll be my honor.

You only have a twenty and the book costs ten. Briefly, you consider leaving nothing, or a note expressing your thanks, knowing there was a time when you would have walked out with the dictionary, and whatever else you could carry, whether you needed it or not; especially if you needed it not. Because need wasn't part of it. Well, maybe a small part. But need had little to do with the object you stole. Need ran deeper then, though you didn't budget for such thoughts.

Then was a long time ago. You were a person you barely remember—a forgotten echo that began way back when and comes booming back around, at last, bouncing off deep canyon walls in a voice you don't understand.

But the ageless face is there, sealed in memory, 4 x 6. So you leave the twenty in the basket and walk out with the Original Portable Tungesa Dictionary under your arm.

You return home and discover a poem of markings on parchment tucked between yellowed pages, and you search the dictionary for the meaning of each stroke.

It's a poem written by a hunter who has given up the hunt, given up all weapons, given up

even the desire to hunt, apparently, but not the desire to discover . . .

And at the bottom of the page in script faintly familiar, you recognize two letters. Initials.

And they
are yours.

WHAT THEY SEE WHEN THEY'RE DYING

Dorothy is dying. Something in Doris' voice tells me before I ask. Huddling near the leafless buckeye, she is skinny shivering against the wood. They give her less than a week. It could be any day, says Doris. Saucers of water and pewter bowls of Borden's condensed milk are all over the house and around the deck. Dorothy's kidney is shot; she's not supposed to have protein, but what the hell, if that's what she wants.

Doris lights a joint and lightly brushes back her white hair. The room grows sweet and gray. She swears that Dorothy's eyes change colors. They see things we don't. She's always said that about cats. Dorothy comes in and springs up onto the bookcase like it was last week when she wasn't supposed to die. *See!* marvels Doris, as Dorothy settles in her usual spot overlooking us. I wonder what they will do with her, what arrangements have been made. Doris wonders how she will live without cat hair after fifteen years.

Saying goodbye to a cat that's not yours is awkward, especially if it's dying. I never knew where I stood with her -- she was that kind of feline. But she doesn't move as my fingers stroke her face. *Someday we'll all be there, says Doris taking Dorothy into her arms, You're just going to be the first one, hon.*

It's upbeat as I go. Who knows, maybe she'll prove everyone wrong. Doris used up all her sick leave and Dorothy didn't die. Cats are tough. Dorothy Mansfield, the old Postmistress was tough. She opened everyone's mail and ran the P.O. at the beach like a prison. That's where they found the skinny tabby, maybe five weeks old.

And back to the beach is where she'll go. Under the apple tree, next to Zoomer -- who didn't zoom fast enough across Highway 1. Dorothy's style is nothing like that. No panic, no frenzied attempt to elude it. She sips water from a little bowl high up and stares over us. I watch her gold eyes but they don't change color. Maybe it's my angle. The lack of light. Smoke. Doris smiles. It's a smile deeply etched in her skin, a smile that hangs on, a smile that knows it must wait.

SS MERCY

The tiny dove drops from the sky and grips the line of a passing sailboat, spreading its damp wings to dry, resting tiny muscles that twitch non-stop. It's a reprieve, an unexpected yet welcome respite, an oasis in the blue vastness—beautiful but without mercy until the sloop appears with a single sailor who smiles at the unexpected company, a hitchhiker who drops in, hangs on, then lifts off. Both bird and sailor going it alone.

REAR VIEW

The dusty truck looks familiar—trailing debris, tarp flapping, tools cinched down with rope. You sold it twenty years ago, tools and all when you went into sales. You pass on the left in your Saab. The young driver smokes a Lucky Strike, one hand on the wheel. You know the gun rack holds loppers and a rod; a basketball rolls around the floorboard; a notebook of poems sits in the glove box. You wanna tell him to quit smoking, buy property in Mill Valley, call mother. You downshift, change lanes. But the truck, a speck in your mirror, draws no closer.

MR. SHORTCUT

I call my boyfriend Apostrophe because he's so possessive.
He calls me Enigma because I'm not. "I'm married," I say.
"Hire a double," he says, "to go through the motions of your life."

But emotions are my bread and butter.

Why hire a Sherpa to pack your gear up the hill?

Dad was Mr. Shortcut. Always after a quicker route to Uncle
Stout's, though he hated iced tea and saying grace before a Sunday
lunch of oniony enchiladas—beneath an abstract watercolor of the
holy trinity painted by his only son Vince one summer in jail.

"Be with me," pleads Apostrophe.
"Stay away," I say—only luring him closer.

We're a pair of docks on a shameless sea. A misplaced metaphor, an ill-conceived pun, a comma coupling two thoughts, trying
to be one.

IN SO MANY WORDS

"**Y**ou're in for a hard rewrite," says Pierre the Cat.

"Metaphorically?" I ask. "Like with this poem? Or life?"

For clarification, he walks across my chest. Licks my earlobe with his sandpaper tongue, his paw catching on my flannel. As if that's supposed to clear things up. It's part of his craft, his editor's technique.

"Why so many words?" he says, but it's not a question.

He takes his time extricating himself from me pinned in my favorite chair, coffee cup just out of reach. Then, with the pen, he settles across my journal and the typed first draft. When Pierre pulls out the pink fine point, adverbs tremble and adjectives pray. I've hidden the red, can you imagine?

"You want to talk about craft," he says, "try writing without any words, without paper. Try living next door to a beginning sax player who doesn't know the beauty of silence." Sometimes Pierre sees metaphor on a different frequency. He looks at me with unblinking yellow eyes. "It takes discipline to write. It takes discipline not to write. You should try it sometime."

He looks away. Licks a spot he missed on his paw.

"Let's be clear on this. If rewriting is getting to know yourself all over again, then let me introduce the two of you..." He yawns.

Pierre has lost all vestiges of his feral origins. But he's a tough-as-nails editor. He leaves the manuscript, hops back on top of me, licks his other paw, his chest, then starts to lick himself down, reaching places I never dreamed of.

"Are you showing off now?" I ask.

He stares at me. Who knows what he sees. Those yellow eyes speak truth. Wordless. That 60-grit tongue rounding odd corners, applying a smooth, fine finish. Showing me how it's done.

"Can I at least refill my coffee cup?" I ask, down to one free hand, my torso under siege. Not a big cat, a dainty killer, in fact, Pierre somehow grows heavy on you. His purring, I take as a no.

Pinned by exponential weight, with his whiskers brushing against my cheek and tickling, I know better than to laugh. His sudden dismounts are 4-claw affairs, and sometimes draw blood— editor's red he calls it, his personal copyediting marks.

"Craft is physical. Catnip is for later. Eating grass is the best way to purge, addition by subtraction. And purge you must," he says, eyeing my manuscript, my words, as he moves to the Istanbul rug and flexes his claws.

"Keep your claws sharp," commands Pierre. "Know when to stop. Work on your indifference. Don't just kill your little darlings as your beloved Faulkner once said. Have a little fun with them, bat them around—scare the precious shit out of them."

Pierre gazes out the window, his back to me. Who knows what he sees. "I once wrote a story," he says, "and it went like this: Pierre walked the streets of Catmandu. Dogs cowered in the shade. Pierre's walking still. End of story."

His tail flicks.

"Every story, every dream, every poem I've written since has been the same, retold. Meaning is a shadow you can't grasp." Pierre saunters into the kitchen. Leaps onto the counter. "Anything made smaller is better—tumors, hairballs, poems. Remember. Anything. Except breakfast. So," he growls, "you got any King Salmon in the house, writer?"

That too is not a question. And so I rise.

ELI NEVER GIVES ADVICE

"If I had any to give, I'd ignore it myself," says Eli. "Steinbeck said that."

Roxie knows this.

She's behind three car payments, her cat's been missing since May, and she might have torn a meniscus.

Eli never interrupts or makes suggestions. His denim blue eyes look colored in.

"Your silences are reassuring, I want you to know," she tells him.

He cracks his jawbone, his one annoying habit, albeit unconscious.

"You're not talking much is like free money to me, Eli. It won't pay my bills, but you're not telling me how to fix an unfixable situation, or telling me not to do something I'd probably do anyway, is just what I need to hear. I feel better. That's all we can hope for, right?"

Eli grins.

Roxie wants to tell him he should start dating again.

But the light in his eyes inspires silence.

In silence she finds love.

WAITING FOR RESULTS

Sitting in the sun on a patio made of stone, I open the dictionary and look up *Benign*. It is already the most beautiful word in the English language. But with that silent g, that way of landing without ending, it sounds as if it alighted from another tongue, perhaps French dropped in for a while and stayed. Some words do that. Was the original name for Butterfly, Flutterby?

Holding the dictionary in my lap I sip green tea and watch a Monarch linger near the bottle brush tree. Butterflies have no mouths but taste through their feet. Some moths never eat, subsisting on stored energy from their youthful larvae days.

These facts are new to me, the way the results of my labs will be. But whatever I have, I've had for a while. Today I'll just find out its name. Which makes today different from yesterday. That, and the way this butterfly now alights on my finger, wings gently pulsing, then flutters away.

EGRET'S FLIGHT

Y ou start with dreams and end up giving them away.

The boat, the trolling motor, the '59 Ford, the MG, the orchard ladder, the pick and shovel, the house, and trailer. They cost you thousands. And you let them go. Give them away to friends, family, strangers, the free bin, Goodwill, the Bank. More stuff arrives to take their place. Books, art, a bike, shirts hardly worn, a vase, certificates with your name on them.

Things pass through that don't belong to you—parades, an egret flying toward you like an arrow, poems by poets you've never heard of, a curator's smile. Dreams that last a moment, an afternoon, a night. Dreams that linger and evaporate, that buoy you, that strike you down, that last until the end of a page, until the end of the earth, until you write them down until the cat licks your nose until you close the book. And this, too, you give away.

FREE VERSE DEPARTURE

Poets bring nothing to the party. They don't even ask. They show up on time or late. They get lost. They say they're coming but don't. They arrive in time for food, stand in a corner, and drink. Never take off their coat. They'll strip to a t-shirt and talk about Bird, things you've never heard as Parker plays on your Alexa. Sometimes poetry breaks out. Someone picks up a guitar. There's action on the roof. Shy cats come out of hiding. An enormous radish gets carved into art. Memory floats up from an afternoon in Oaxaca, 1984. The houseboat rises, warms. Everyone leaves all at once in a free verse departure. Sink full of dishes. Someone leaves a hat. The night itself becomes a poem. That's what the poets brought.

"Keep searchin' for your mystery note on the universal piano of life."

RAHSAAN ROLAND KIRK

READING GUIDE

If I had more time, I'd write a shorter story.

Mark Twain

It's tricky business—how much to include and how much to leave out when writing short fiction. That's part of the craft. Micros and flash are close cousins of prose poems. They're spare, they rely on metaphor, vivid imagery, and language. And they're short. While specific word counts vary from publisher to publisher, micros are usually under 400 words, while flash fiction runs up to 1,000. Subgenres include the well-known six-word stories, 100-word stories, and even six-sentence stories.

Techniques to hone one-inch punch fiction include time limits, word limits, and surface limits, too. Composing on an envelope, a grocery list, or a cocktail napkin, affects not only what you write but how much you include, as well.

THINK INSIDE THE BOX. Use restrictions as tools to discover how to express more with less.

Here are some writing seeds to try:

- Make a list of opening sentences and titles. Choose one and write for ten minutes.
- Choose a one or two-page story you've written and reduce it to 100 words exactly.

Representative stories: "Glass Man" (p. 14), "Rear View" (p. 79)

A STORY IS OFTEN DESCRIBED AS something that happens to someone, somewhere . . . and I would add—so what?!

- Make a short list of places: Café Trieste, Niagara Falls, Bullhead City, Salzburg, jail . . . and write on the back of an envelope or postcard; see where it takes you.

Representative stories: "Headlong" (p. 49), "Short Walk on a Long Pier" (p. 68)

WRITE FIRST DRAFTS without limits or edits and reduce in the rewrite. Learn what cuts strengthen a story and make your sentences more sinewy. Reduce or eliminate adjectives and adverbs where you can. They often serve as unnecessary qualifiers. Where possible, avoid explanations and chunks of flow-interrupting backstory, too. If need be, craft information into dialog and have a character deliver the goods.

Representative stories: "So Many Words" (p. 81)

Hemingway believed you could take out what you know, once written, and the reader will still feel it, intuit it as if it's still on the page. But if you leave out something you don't know, it creates a hole in the story. This is one of the mysteries of craft, a discovery we make along the way in our apprenticeship of this astonishing genre-bending form.

Part of the power and the appeal of the short form is how it evokes rather than explains. Leaving space between the lines for the reader, as I mentioned in the intro, provides opportunities for readers to sync with a story and have their own *Aha* moments. This can create a profound connection, and together, the reader and writer may create something new that may not even be on the page.

Sometimes micros and flash don't end—at least not in the traditional way—they land. This is another way to extend the story by allowing the narrative possibilities to continue beyond words on a page.

I never look for answers when I read fiction, I seek understanding. Answers can reduce and restrict, and sometimes they're wrong (!), while understanding broadens the range of possibilities. Imagine turning all the lights on in your house and walking across the street to see how you live. That's what writing micros and flash is like for me, even, of course, when it's fiction.

Because, as Fellini said, "All art is autobiographical; the pearl is the oyster's autobiography."

"*Every story I write adds to me a little, changes me a little, forces me to reexamine an attitude or belief, causes me to research and learn, helps me to understand people and grow... Every story I create creates me. I write to create myself.*"

OCTAVIA BUTLER

ACKNOWLEDGMENTS

Thank you to the following publications where some of these stories first appeared: *MacQueen's Quinterly, Riddled with Arrows, Carve Magazine, Bull, Flashback Fiction, KYSO FLASH, The Disappointed Housewife, Come & Go Literary, Ruminate, Nomadic Press, The Sea Letter, HOOT, Exposition Review, Medusa's Laugh Press, Map Literary, Exposition Review, Alchemy, Pacific Sun, Peeking Cat Literary, Pretty Owl Poetry, Third Wednesday, great weather for MEDIA, Civil Liberties United, Pocket Lint, and Flash Frontier.*

And thank you to J. K. Fowler, Michaela Mullin, Jevohn Tyler Newsome, and the Nomadic family for supporting my work and the work of so many writers and artists; for providing venues and platforms for voices to be heard and craft to be shared; for creating opportunities to be generous, gracious, and kind.

Thank you to editor Nina Sacco for her keen eye, kindness, and brilliance. Thank you to James, Dan, Meg, Joyce, Norma, Kara, Robert, Kevin, Jim, Veronica, Linda, Tony, and J. Martin Strangeweather for reading my work and providing your kind words. Thank you to Norm, Florencia, Tony Aldarondo, and Steven. Thank you to Naz, Sevan, Kim, and Sandy. Thank you, Tongo. Thank you to Rebecca, Ken, and Betty. Thanks to all my students. Thank you Ruth, Drew & Jenn, Penny & Ruthie, Tu & Emmie, and Betty Ann. Rex and Roy. Thank you, sweet Phyllis. And thank you, readers, for joining the dance.

Guy Biederman

Guy Biederman is the author of six collections of short work, including *Nova Nights, Edible Grace, Soundings* and *Fathoms*. His work has appeared in many journals including *Carve, Flashback Fiction, Bull, Flash Frontier,* and *MacQueen's Quinterly*. Biederman's fiction and poetry has won a Publisher's Choice Award, an Editor's Choice Award, been nominated for Best of the Net, and won 3rd place in New Zealand's National Flash Fiction contest. Born in the Chihuahuan desert, raised on a stingray in Ventura, Biederman learned to write while living in a goat herder's shack during a civil war in Guatemala. He lives on a houseboat with his wife and salty cat and walks the planks daily.

🌐 www.guybiederman.com

COVER MISSIVE

On "Words for an untitled map (no. 13-11)"

by Thérèse Murdza

I make the paintings and I think of you. The still pandemic. Alive. For some. Together. For some, with ink and pigment, a woven slow act between us and time and boundless Intimacy. Geography. Science and care.

Today is an ordinary day. An extraordinary day.

What is possible here?
What do you see?

A tangle of soot black linings running the ground and pushing into open parts of mourning? The red of horizon? A pink that requires something of you. These white blue green gold spaces and shapes and oranges. Bright and generous. Pieces of fate.

I am reading aloud to you. There is no alone. Not really. Hands, if you have them, will always need washing. The shape of your face, half-masked, is still beautiful.

The new is here anyway. Any way. Anyway.
The new is here anyway. Any way. New.

⊙ tmurdza.studioart

4 OTHER WAYS TO
SUPPORT
NOMADIC PRESS
WRITERS

Please consider supporting these funds. You can donate on a one-time or monthly basis from $10–∞ You can also more generally support Nomadic Press by donating to our general fund via nomadicpress.org/donate and by continuing to buy our books.

As always, thank you for your support!

Scan the QR code for more information and/or to donate.

You can also donate at nomadicpress.org/store.

ABOUT THE FUNDS

**XALAPA
FUND**

XALAPA FUND

The Xalapa Fund was started in May of 2022 to help offset the airfare costs of Nomadic Press authors to travel to our new retreat space in Xalapa, Veracruz in Mexico. Funds of up to $350 will be dispersed to any Nomadic Press published author who wishes to travel to Xalapa. The funds are kept in a separate bank account and disbursements are overseen by three (3) Nomadic Press authors and Founding Publisher J. K. Fowler.

Inherent in these movements will be cultural exchanges and Nomadic Press will launch a reading series based out of the bookstore/cafe downstairs from the space in August 2022. This series will feature Xalapa-based writers and musicians as well as open-mic slots and will be live streamed to build out relationships between our communities in Oakland, California, Philadelphia, Pennsylvania, and the greater US (and beyond).

EMERGENCY FUND

Right before Labor Day 2020 (and in response to the effects of COVID), Nomadic Press launched its Emergency Fund, a forever fund meant to support Nomadic Press-published writers who have no income, are unemployed, don't qualify for unemployment, have no healthcare, or are just generally in need of covering unexpected or impactful expenses.

Funds are first come, first serve, and are available as long as there is money in the account, and there is a dignity centered internal application that interested folks submit. Disbursements are made for any amount up to $300. All donations made to this fund are kept in a separate account. The Nomadic Press Emergency Fund (NPEF) account and associated processes (like the application) are overseen by Nomadic Press authors and the group meets every month.

BLACK WRITERS FUND

On nineteenth (June 19) 2020, Nomadic Press launched the Nomadic Press Black Writers Fund (NPBWF), a forever fund that will be directly built into the fabric of our organization for as long as Nomadic Press exists and puts additional monies directly into the pockets of our Black writers at the end of each year.

Here is how it works: $1 of each book sale goes into the fund. At the end of each year, all Nomadic Press authors have the opportunity to voluntarily donate none, part, or all of their royalties to the fund. Anyone from our larger communities can donate to the fund. This is where you come in! At the end of the year, whatever monies are in the fund will be evenly distributed to all Black Nomadic Press authors that have been published by the date of disbursement (mid-to-late December). The fund (and associated, separate bank account) has an oversight team comprised of four authors (Ayodele Nzinga, Daniel B. Summerhill, Dazié Grego-Sykes, and Odelia Younge) + Nomadic Press Executive Director J. K. Fowler

PAINTING THE STREETS FUND

The Nomadic Press Painting the Streets Fund was launched in February 2022 to support visual arts programs in Oakland flatlands' schools. Its launch coincided with the release of *Painting the Streets: Oakland Uprising in the Time of Rebellion*. Your donations here will go directly into a separate bank account overseen by J. K. Fowler (Nomadic Press), Elena Serrano (Eastside Arts Alliance), Leslie Lopez (EastSide Arts Alliance), Rachel Wolfe-Goldsmith (BAMP), and Andre Jones (BAMP). In addition, all net proceeds from the sale of *Painting the Streets: Oakland Uprising in the Time of Rebellion* will go into this fund.

We will share the fund's impact annually on project partner websites. Here are a few schools that we have already earmarked to receive funds: _le Omode, Madison High School, McClymonds High School, Roosevelt Middle School, Elmhurst Middle School, Castlemont High School, Urban Promise Academy, West Oakland Middle School, and POC Homeschoolers of Oakland.